ONE-osaurus, TWO-osaurus

Kim Norman

illustrated by Pierre Collet-Derby

CANDLEWICK PRESS

For Eugene and Harvey,
who really count!
KN

For Wes
PC-D

First edition 2021. Library of Congress Catalog Card Number 2021933627. ISBN 978-1-5362-0179-6. This book was typeset in Burbank Big Regular. The illustrations were created digitally. Candlewick Press, 99 Dover Street, Somerville, Massachusetts 02144. www.candlewick.com
Printed in Shenzhen, Guangdong, China. 21 22 23 24 25 CCP 10 9 8 7 6 5 4 3 2

One misty, moisty morning,
long before the world was tame . . .

some prehistoric pals set out
to play a counting game.

One-osaurus,

two-osaurus . . .

three-osaurus,

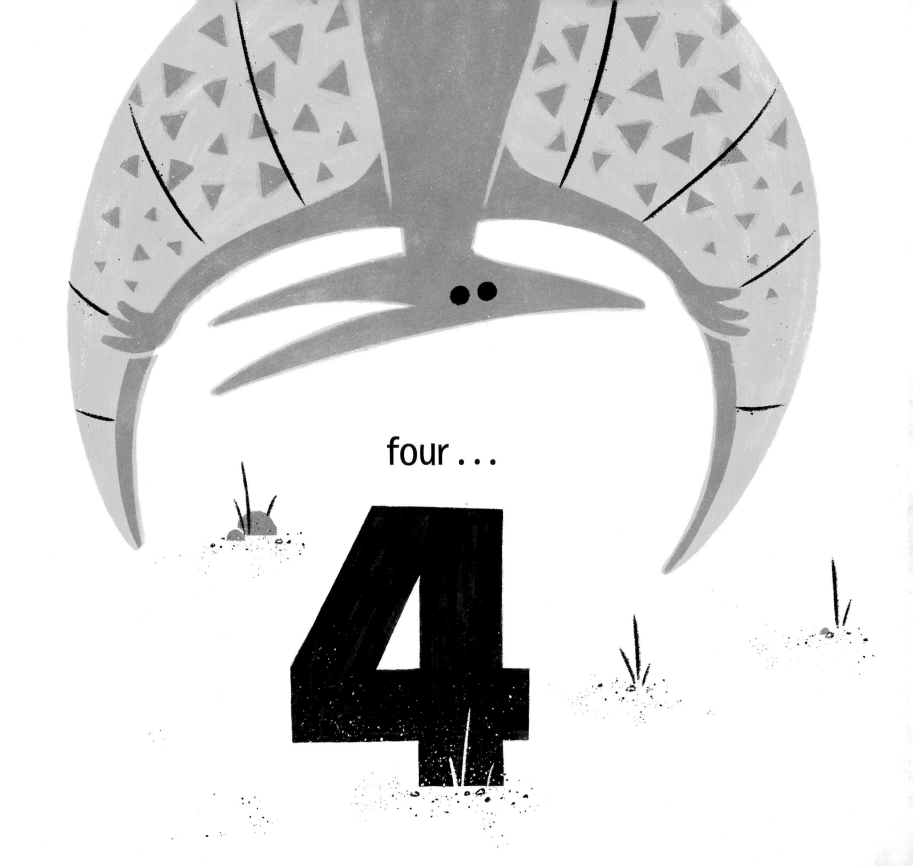

four . . .

five-osaurus,

six-osaurus,

seven-osaurus . . .

7

Something's coming –
something big!
No one say a word!

Rumble. Rattle.

Quick, skedaddle –
raptor in the lead.

"Ready or not, here I come!"

Dinosaur stampede!

Everybody quiet now.

Tuck your tails and necks.

Closer, closer . . .

Time is up!

It's ten-osaurus rex!

Chomp-osaurus, stomp-osaurus.
Sniffle . . . snuffle . . . sneak.

Ready? Here he is –
the mighty . . .

CHOMP!

KING
of hide-and-seek!

ROAR!

One by one
they're found-osaurus,
even clever four.

Time to play a different game . . .

like Simon Says-osaur!

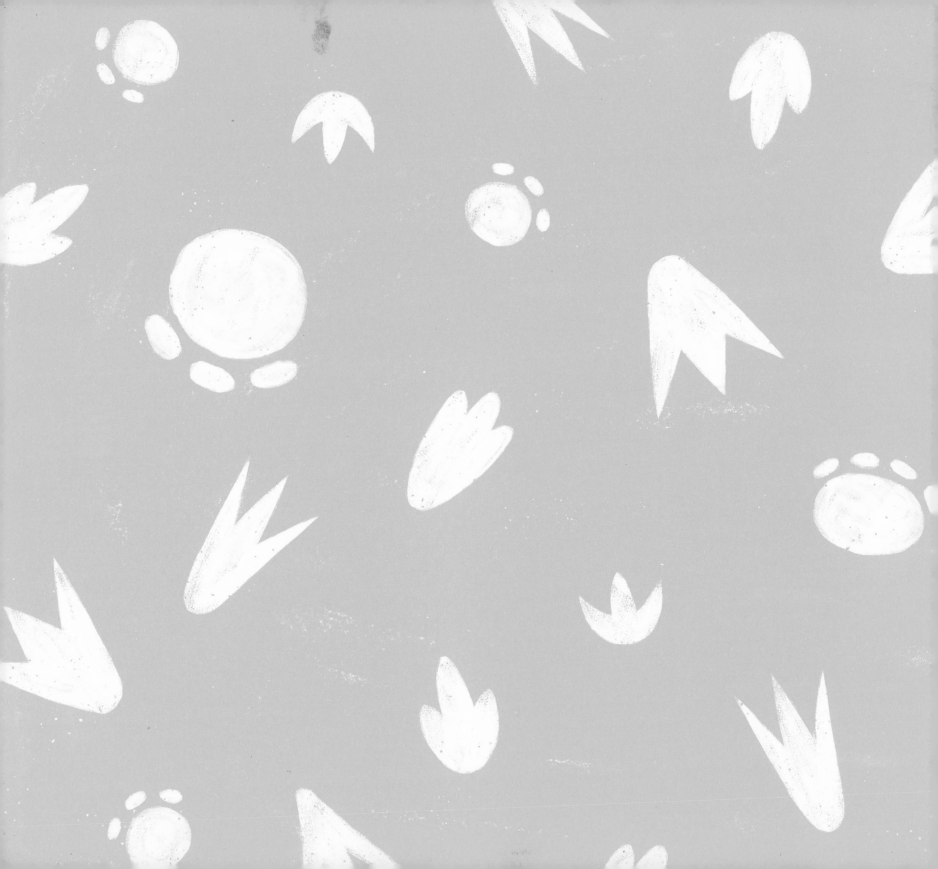